THE STAR CHASER

The Star Chaser

June Wang

PREFACE

Life is like an unending journey, vast and boundless at times, deep and mysterious at others. Each of us is like a seeker of stars, carrying a vague yet steadfast yearning as we tread unknown paths, searching for that faint yet radiant light—a metaphor for the dreams and aspirations we hold close.

Our hearts are often filled with contradictions and conflicts: we crave security but yearn for freedom; we fear solitude yet need it to confront ourselves; we pursue light but are often entangled by the darkness within. Every phase of life feels like a dialogue with oneself—a constant confrontation with desires, fears, illusions, and truths.

From childhood, we are handed a "box." Within this box lie rules, safety, passive growth, and silent constraints. It shapes our initial understanding of the world while planting the seeds of a desire to break free and grow. We grow accustomed to the comfort of the box, as it offers certainty and familiarity. Yet, the box also distances us from ourselves, eroding our courage to explore the unknown. Psychologist Carl Jung once introduced the concept of "individuation," suggesting that life's task is to integrate consciousness and the unconscious, to embrace the shadows within, and ultimately become whole. Breaking open the box and embarking on the journey to seek the stars is, in truth, a metaphorical process of exploring our inner selves and reshaping who we are.

This book is about stories of "stepping out"—about those who, though lonely yet resolute, chase their dreams, represented by the stars. Along the path of pursuing dreams, we encounter various people and experiences—some that lead us astray, some that awaken us, and some that offer a thread of solace and warmth in the depths of despair. All of these moments remind us: to achieve true growth and freedom, we must face our shadows and embrace our imperfect but authentic selves.

These stories are not written to provide you with definitive answers, but to embark on a shared exploration:

- How do we find inner peace and strength amidst confusion and solitude?
- How do we accept our insecurities and vulnerabilities, allowing our authentic selves to emerge through the fractures and rebuild stronger?

May you find your own star within these pages, whether it shines in a far-off sky or has been quietly residing within your heart all along.

June Wang

DEDICATION

To the self who once sought light in the
darkness,
To the child who gazed at the stars, brim-
ming with curiosity,
To the grown-ups who still dare to chase
dreams barefoot.

CONTENTS

ONE

HIDDEN IN THE BOX

I am someone hidden inside a box. It was not until I stepped out of the box that I truly understood this.

The box was perfectly square, made of corrugated cardboard, gray-brown in color, measuring 50 centimeters on each side, and 5 millimeters thick.

You might wonder, how can I describe it so precisely? I spent countless hours inside that box immersed in mathematics, philosophy, and physics, drawing geometric patterns. I even practiced until I could draw perfect circles and equilateral triangles by hand, without using a compass.

Since childhood, I've lived inside this box, surrounded by formulas, charts, and words filled with "rules." No one ever told me why I needed to learn these things—it just seemed like the "right thing to do."

At the center of the box's top was a thin slit, about 50 centimeters long.

During the day, a golden ray of light would shine through the slit, piercingly bright, falling directly onto my face.

Through this light, I observed the box's material: the rough, gray-brown surface of the paper, densely printed with words. Borrowing the light, I diligently studied the formulas and rules within the box, though I never understood their purpose.

Occasionally, a breeze would drift through the slit, carrying yellow dust; sometimes, it brought the faint scent of rain.

At night, everything turned dark. Occasionally, a faint, soft white light would spill through the slit, accompanied by the distant songs of insects serenading their mates.

The box was a safe and warm place. I would curl up to sleep, kneel to think, and sometimes daydream: "What could be outside the slit? Another box, perhaps?" But whenever my hand reached out toward the slit and I saw the words on the box, I would quickly pull my fingers back—

**"Warning: The outside is danger-
ous. You will face countless unknown fears!"**

At that moment, I would tell myself:
"It's wrong for me to keep thinking about
what's outside the slit. I live in the box;
the box protects me, and I must obey its
rules. This is the way my world is meant
to be."

Sometimes, I would wonder: could the
outside be the same—filled with "prohibi-
tions," "musts," and "should," but never a
"why"?

Until one day, a white seed with a
fluffy parachute squeezed through the
slit.

It introduced itself as a dandelion, and
many of the stories about the outside
world were told to me by it.

"Though I am a child of the sun and the
wind, I am no ordinary dandelion," it said
proudly. "I lived under a giant tree. My
mother told us to fly toward the nearby
stream and forest so we could continue

our comfortable lives. All my siblings obeyed, but I was born rebellious! I am a dandelion who loves gazing at the stars."

"Stars?" I asked curiously. "What are those?"

The dandelion looked at me with disdain, its white fluff trembling. "You ignorant creature living in a box—you don't even know what stars are!"

I felt ashamed, as if I had missed out on the most mysterious and beautiful thing in the world.

"Stars come in many colors—yellow, white, blue, red, purple, even green. They are embedded in large signs, forming beautiful words. They also appear inside a huge black concrete box. Many people collect stars, take them home, chat with them, dance and sing under their light. It's so lively!"

The dandelion grew more excited as it spoke, its fluff trembling slightly. "These are the sights the passing birds told me about—scenes I've never seen but must be stunning! Yet my mother says that what I described are not stars at all and that they are dangerous and could kill me!"

"What? So dangerous?" I was startled, instinctively curling up. "Then why do you still like them?"

The dandelion smiled; its voice filled with determination. "People often deny their dreams out of fear of the unknown, then drown in mundane, tiresome lives, lamenting that they've lost their dreams. I refuse to be like that! I am a free dandelion. I love adventure. If I love something, not even death can stop me from flying toward it! Had the wind not blown me off course, I would already be in the world of stars by now!"

The dandelion's words filled me with both shame and admiration. I wanted to help it in some way.

So, we discussed wind resistance, gravity, its flight speed, and distance. We planned to help it achieve its dream of flying toward the stars on a windy day.

One morning, as a southeastern wind blew, the dandelion was ready to depart.

"I feel full of strength!" it said excitedly. "Goodbye, my friend! Chasing dreams is exhilarating! I hope one day you, too, will open your box for something and see the vibrant world outside. If you ever reach a place full of stars and see the most beautiful swaying dandelion, that will be me!"

I cupped it in my hand and let it pass through the slit. The wind lifted the dandelion, carrying it far away until it disappeared into the light.

From that day on, it felt as though a slit had appeared in my heart as well. A bright beam of light shone through, burning me intensely.

The palms of my hands and the soles of my feet felt hot and restless, and my heart pounded uncontrollably.

I began losing focus, easily distracted. When I came back to my senses, I would find my hand stroking the light that streamed in, or even the dust floating in the air.

At night, I couldn't sleep, often shedding inexplicable tears. The tears soaked the bottom of the box, softening the cardboard. Without thinking, I pressed down with my hand and accidentally poked a small hole. Startled, I pulled my hand back, noticing that my fingertips were stained with black soil and carried a damp, grassy scent.

All of this terrified me, yet it also gave me a faint sense that the world beyond the box was calling to me.

TWO

THE STAR ARRIVES

One night, the sound of wings flapping came from the slit in the box, accompanied by a faint, flickering light.

"Who are you?" I asked curiously.

"I am a star," a soft, tender voice replied. Through the slit, I caught glimpses of two antennae and a pair of black eyes. "Where are you? I can't see you," it continued.

"I'm right here. I'm a person living in this enclosed space," I answered.

"Oh, poor thing! How boring your life must be! Come out and admire my beautiful figure! I dare say you've never seen a star as radiant as me," it declared with a proud, almost boastful tone.

"I can't get out. There are no windows or doors, and the walls are too sturdy," I muttered. It was an excuse, really. Thankfully, the box hid my face, flushed with embarrassment.

"This isn't a house; it's just a soft box! Someone as strong as me could easily tear it apart!"

Two slender claws reached through the slit, scratching and pulling at it for ages, but the slit didn't budge. Out of breath, it stopped and said, "Are you just too scared to come out? Don't worry, with me here, it's completely safe! I'm incredibly strong and stunning!"

I remained silent.

That night, however, I slept unusually well and even dreamed. In the dream, there was a radiant light that filled me with happiness.

The next day, it came again. Through the slit, its faint yellow glow sparkled softly.

"Isn't my light beautiful? Do you know how many people fight over me?"

Listening to its boastful voice, I couldn't help but laugh. "Yes, indeed, you are the most beautiful star I've ever seen."

It was overjoyed, hopping excitedly on top of the box. I could even hear its light footsteps. After a while, it coughed and solemnly declared, "You have excellent taste! I've decided—you now have the honor of being my best friend."

I had a friend! And such a delightful little one. Though it loved to brag and was rather fragile, you have to understand—when you're a lonely person living in a box, having a glowing "star" solemnly declare you its best friend is something so tender and heartwarming.

The third day, the fourth day, the fifth day... the sixth day, it came at the same time each day, glowing and sparkling, singing, dancing, and proudly chatting about its vast knowledge of the world.

My heart began to find peace. I stopped crying and no longer struggled to fall asleep. Every day, before the time of its arrival, I would sit quietly, head tilted up, gazing at the slit, eagerly awaiting its return.

I thought, living in the box isn't so bad after all. It's safe here, and I have an adorable friend who visits me every day.

On the seventh day, its light began to dim, and its voice grew faint.

"My dear friend, I have to go," it said.

"Where are you going?" My heart suddenly raced, and a sense of unease surged within me.

"My mission on land is coming to an end. I'm returning to the world of stars," it said weakly, the sound of its wings barely audible.

"Before I leave, I want to give you a gift."

"What gift?" I asked eagerly.

"The gift is by the edge of your box. I couldn't fit it through the slit," it paused, then added softly, "I've enjoyed talking to you. The fact that we've never met kept our connection spiritual and mysterious. But I've also thought—if one day, you step out of the box for me, I'd feel truly special, as if I'd accomplished something extraordinary. Perhaps all the stars around me would even admire me."

"Are you leaving here to join those stars?"

"Yes. Even among so many stars, I'll still be the brightest and strongest," it said with a proud laugh.

After a moment of silence, it added softly, "I'm sorry."

"Why are you apologizing?" I asked, puzzled.

"I lied. I'm not the brightest star. I'm small and weak, and no one has ever liked me," it said sadly, then fell silent again.

My heart tightened, and I blurted out, "I like you. You're my best friend."

Suddenly, I wanted to step out and hug it. I began pushing against the slit with my body, clawing at the edges of the box.

"I'm very lonely. You're my best friend on Earth," it said with a small laugh. "My only friend, really."

The walls of the box grew thinner. Dust fell, making me cough.

"In this world, I have the body of an insect. It's not beautiful, and I've always felt ashamed of it. I knew you couldn't come out, so I lied to you," its voice continued.

I tore at the box desperately, sensing it was about to leave.

"I don't want you to see me as I am now. I'm afraid you'd think I'm ugly," it sighed softly. "But once I return to my starry form, everything will be fine. When you reach the world's brightest, most beautiful star and bring the gift I left you, I'll recognize you."

Outside, the voice suddenly disappeared.

At last, I tore open the top of the box.

There was nothing terrifying outside—no stars, no sign of the insect.

A breeze blew in, slightly chilly. In the eastern sky, orange sunlight poured down, wrapping me gently.

Looking down, I saw a few small, dark brown seeds at the edge of the box. They looked like tiny plant seeds, perhaps the "gift" it left behind.

I turned to look at the place I'd lived. It was a square, gray-brown corrugated cardboard box, roughly 50 centimeters long, wide, and tall, and only 5 millimeters thick.

The warning on the box— "Warning: The outside is dangerous. You will face countless unknown fears!"—was now ripped into jagged fragments scattered on the ground.

I gently placed the seeds into the pocket over my chest.

Then, I took my first step out of the box.

THREE

THE BOUQUET

From that day onward, I left the box I had lived in for what felt like an eternity and stepped into the outside world.

I pressed my foot gently into the ground, which felt soft and warm, carrying the damp scent of soil. Looking around, the space stretched vast and empty. I didn't know which direction to take my first step.

Turning to a nearby bush, I asked, "Excuse me, which way should I go?"

The bush stood still, aloof and indifferent, giving no response.

"Rustle, rustle—" A cluster of birch trees suddenly began to sway, whispering among themselves. I looked up at them and shouted, "Can you tell me which direction will lead me to the stars?"

The birches swayed their branches, brushing against one another, and eventually, all their treetops pointed in the same direction.

At that moment, a powerful yet gentle breeze came from behind me, nudging me forward, making me stumble as I moved ahead.

Passing through the woods, the trees and grasses thinned out, revealing a narrow dirt path paved with yellow earth. The ground was firm, and the path was marked with various footprints: human steps, hoof prints, paw marks, and others I couldn't recognize.

"Hey... hey..." A faint voice called out.

Following the sound, I saw something purple lying on the ground about twenty meters ahead. I hurried over, dust kicking up around me, gilding my feet and pants with a golden edge.

It was a bouquet of purple flowers. Six broken stems were tied together with a piece of brown twine. Dust clung to the petals, which trembled faintly as the bouquet let out a weak call for help.

"Are you okay?" I carefully cradled it in my hands and asked softly.

"I... I'm really not okay," it sobbed. "My leaves are parched, gasping for air, and my petals have become brittle and dry. I think... my fate is not what my name suggests. This is the second time my lover has abandoned me."

"Maybe there's a stream or a pond nearby. I can take you there to get some water!" I offered urgently.

"No," the bouquet quivered slightly but spoke firmly. "I no longer have roots. Even if I drink water now, I'd only live another day or two. I want you to take me to my lover and ask him why he abandoned me. Follow this path until you reach the largest tree—there's a wooden house beneath it. That's where he is."

Holding the purple bouquet carefully, I avoided brushing against its fragile petals. The petals were as thin as paper, emitting a soft, faint rustling sound with each tiny tremor, as if they might tear at any moment.

After about fifteen minutes of walking, I came across a small garden. The garden was empty of blooming flowers, scattered only with bare roots and broken leaves. Beside it stood a large, lush tree, and on the tree sat a simple wooden house.

Underneath the tree, a little boy with his head bowed sat slumped on the ground, looking dejected.

"Sorry to bother you, but do you recognize this bouquet?" I asked gently as I approached him.

The boy looked up at the bouquet in my hands. The moment he saw the flowers, his furrowed brow lifted slightly, and a small smile appeared at the corners of his mouth. Reaching out, he asked in surprise, "Didn't she go to the forest? Where did you find her?"

"By the roadside. She's on the verge of withering."

"Oh, quickly put her in this bottle!" The boy scrambled up to the treehouse, bringing down a water bottle. Carefully, he poured half the water into it and placed the purple bouquet inside.

The bouquet absorbed the water, its petals softening slightly, but it still seemed to struggle for breath, as if it hadn't fully recovered from its desiccation.

Looking at the boy, I asked softly, "The bouquet wants to ask you—why do you keep abandoning her?"

The boy froze, then responded in confusion, "Why would I abandon her? From the time she was a seed, I patiently sowed her, waited for her to sprout and grow leaves. I weeded and fertilized her, nurturing her until she grew taller and more beautiful than the other flowers.

Then, when she bloomed, a wealthy boy from town came and said he wanted to take her to his grand home. His house is huge, with a lake in the backyard, while I'm just a poor boy with only this tiny treehouse. I thought she'd have a better life there... so I let him take her."

"And then? Did she come back to you?"

The boy nodded and continued, "Yes. I missed her so much that I would secretly peek at her through the window. But one day, I saw the wealthy boy bringing home a new bouquet of bright, dazzling flowers, while my flower was left discarded at the door. I brought her back, feeling both heartbroken and a little angry—angry that she wasn't as vibrant and radiant as the other flowers, angry that she couldn't win the wealthy boy's favor.

Later, a bird came. It told me that flowers yearn for freedom and offered to take my flower to the skies, to the forest, to scatter her seeds in the freest of places. I thought, how poor I was, with only this small garden—I couldn't confine her... so I agreed to let the bird take her."

The boy sighed and lowered his head. "But I didn't expect that bird to leave her by the roadside."

The bouquet trembled slightly, its voice soft and sorrowful. "But that's not what I wanted..."

I looked down at the bouquet and asked gently, "What is it that you want?"

The flower gazed at the boy, its expression one of sorrow and grievance. "I want you to stay by my side, to quietly watch me grow, bloom, bear seeds, and wither. I want to live my life fully, in my own way. If you're willing, when the pests come, help me drive them away; when the storms arrive, help prop up my branches. If you can just do these simple things, I'll be utterly happy."

But the boy didn't seem to hear the flower's words. He looked at me, bewildered, and said, "You're asking what I want? I want her to bloom brilliantly in a grand, sunlit estate or castle. I want her to be the most precious flower in the world. I don't want her to live like me, stuck in this barren land with a broken house."

I looked at him, then at the bouquet, and said softly, "Flower, he doesn't understand your words or your feelings. He's lost in his own self-loathing and projects his dreams onto you. I think living with a lover who can't communicate is very painful. Will you come with me?"

The flower shook its head gently and whispered, "No, I won't leave him. I know his self-righteous love has hurt me time and again. But I still don't want to give up. I want to try again, to try talking to him once more. I hate him, but I also love him deeply."

The flower and I bid farewell to the boy and left the garden.

After a few steps, I stopped and turned back to ask the boy, "Can you tell me this flower's name? I want to remember her."

The boy paused from his work tending the garden, looked up, and said, "This flower is called Forget-Me-Not."

Perhaps next year, this garden will bloom with many new purple flowers.

But you know what?

Those little flowers will be her, and yet not her.

FOUR

THE CAT

"Excuse me, lonely traveler, have you seen a black cat with bright yellow eyes on your journey?"

A young woman leaned against a sturdy tree, tilting her head slightly as she smiled at me. She wore a black cloak, her hair draping loosely over her shoulders, partially obscuring her eyes. Only half of her languid yet elegant face was visible. Beside her was a tall black bicycle, with a wrinkled black cloth bag hanging from it, worn by time.

Sunlight filtered through the leaves, dappled on her figure, swaying like shadows on a canvas. She seemed like a character from an enigmatic and graceful painting.

I approached her cautiously, standing before her as I hesitantly asked, "A cat? I've never seen such an animal. Could you tell me what it looks like?"

She raised her eyebrows, her smile deepening. "A cat, you ask? It's a sensitive yet wild creature. They have big eyes whose pupils change with the light and bodies so soft they seem like liquid. Oh, and," she added with a playful glint in her eye, "you can exchange your story for a story about the cat."

I thought for a moment and then shared with her the story of the dandelion I had met, ending in a quiet voice, "I'm looking for the stars."

"Stars?" The woman paused, then suddenly laughed so hard that she bent over, coughing between breaths. She patted her chest, trying to catch her breath, and said, "Is it the kind of stars the dandelion told you about? Silly child, if you keep walking, you'll eventually reach a place with many tall concrete buildings. Sit on a bench in the central cement garden, and you'll see the kind of stars you described. But I think those aren't the ones you're searching for."

When her laughter faded, her expression turned serious. Leaning back against the tree trunk, she said slowly, "Let me tell you the story of the cat."

Her voice was soft and low, as though her memories were a deep well filled with sediment from the past.

"When I was your age, I was a little witch recklessly wandering the cement world."

"You might think witches cast spells, ride broomsticks, and know countless mysterious incantations. But in truth, I was just a pitiful little nobody with a shabby broomstick and no magic to speak of, drifting alone on the city's corners. I felt like the whole world didn't love me, not even myself. I thought I was just a speck of dust in the air, ready to disappear at any moment."

She paused, letting out a self-deprecating laugh. "Perhaps lonely people always want to hide themselves, yet deep inside, they're desperate for someone to notice them."

"One day, a boy walked to the corner bakery and saw me wandering there, hungry. He handed me a cookie and a slice of bread. He said he wanted to save me and take me to a place where hunger didn't exist.

The first day, I thought he was a liar.

The second day, I thought he was a fool.

But after a month of him coming every day, I began to feel like an ungrateful, venomous beggar."

"I couldn't hold back my anger and shouted at him, 'I don't need your self-righteous kindness or salvation!' Then, I rode my broomstick and flew away."

"On the roadside, I saw a black cat leaning against a garbage can. Its matted fur clung to its emaciated body, and its golden-yellow eyes shone like stars trapped in darkness.

I frowned, seeing the cookie the boy had given me crushed into crumbs in my hand. After hesitating, I tossed the crumbs to the cat.

To my surprise, with its tearful eyes, it stubbornly followed me home."

Her voice grew softer. She paused and sighed before continuing, "Ah, it was such a troublesome little thing. I was so disgusted by how dirty it was that I took it to a fountain to give it a bath. That's when I discovered a thin scar running along its body, deeply embedded beneath its fur. When I touched it, it winced in pain, tears streaming from its eyes. Yet, it kept gazing at me with those damp, gentle eyes, letting me roughly scrub it without flinching."

"It was so strange. How could such a cold, obsessive, and erratic person like me be met with such patience and kindness from this cat?"

Her gaze turned melancholic as she continued, "One day, on a street corner, I saw a familiar figure—it was him. He shyly handed flowers to another girl. I panicked and fell from the sky. It was my scrappy little cat who called on a group of other cats to drag me back to my shabby shed. In its desperation, the scar on its body split open, and tiny beads of blood seeped out.

I held it in my arms, my eyes dry and aching, yet no tears fell. But there it was—my scrappy little cat crying again. Such a little crybaby."

"'Why are you so good to me?' I asked it many times. But it would only look up, its bright eyes unblinking, as if it were silently saying it loved me unconditionally."

The woman smiled faintly, though her voice carried a subtle tremor. "Back then, I would take it on my broomstick, flying over gray high-rises and through forgotten alleys. It clung tightly to the broomstick's handle, never letting go, no matter how strong the wind blew."

Her voice grew husky. "I was just a reckless little witch back then, bony and silent, pretending to be a renowned sorceress hidden in the world. My favorite pastime was scaring human children sucking on lollipops, just to see them drop their candy and run away in fear."

Her smile slowly faded, and her gaze dimmed. "But my insecurity and self-doubt crept into my heart. After feeling its love, I began to fear it might leave me, that it didn't belong to me, that it might stop loving me. I threw all my loneliness, anger, and insecurity at it. I commanded it to belong to me, to only have eyes for me, to never leave my side.

But it was such a mischievous creature! Whenever I wasn't paying attention, it would sneak out and return late at night. One day, I was so furious that I threw it against the wall with reddened eyes. It got up, whimpered softly, and never dared to jump back into my lap again."

She lowered her head, her voice barely audible. "The next morning, it was gone. I searched everywhere it might have gone, but I realized I didn't even know where it liked to go."

Her voice quivered slightly. "I crouched on the street corner, covering my face as I cried, muttering 'I'm sorry,' but it really was gone, leaving no trace behind.

Later, I abandoned my broomstick and spells, becoming a maid and living as an ordinary human. For a while, I played the role of someone with emotions, a family, and friends.

Later still, I became a bard, telling its story to many people."

"On this journey, I've seen many cats by the roadside. I give them cookies but never take any home. My bag is filled with food and toys I've prepared for it."

A tear slipped from her eye as she whispered, "I miss it so much."

With that, the woman slowly stood, gently brushing the dust from her cloak.

"Thank you for listening to my story." She glanced back at me, her voice soft and fading, "Lonely traveler, may you find your star."

The wind lifted her cloak, rustling the branches, as her figure gradually disappeared down the tree-lined path. For a fleeting moment, I thought I saw her shadow transform into a black cat—its ears slightly perked, its movements fluid like water, perfectly blending with her story.

"So... she was the cat?" I murmured, watching her silhouette dissolve into the wind.

FIVE

DANDELION

Walking forward along this path, I saw towering concrete buildings rising in the distance. Like colossal pillars, they stood upright against the gray, misty sky, as though they were holding the entire city up to the heavens.

As dusk fell, the steel forest began to light up. Neon lights in every hue adorned the façades of the skyscrapers, their flickering brilliance dancing through the air, bringing life to the cold, lifeless city.

I arrived at the center of a cement-paved garden and sat down slowly.

In this small space, a few wilting roses bowed their heads, their drooping leaves like weathered souls sighing quietly. Around me, the rush of traffic roared, and people hurried by, oblivious to the modest garden in their midst.

Then, my gaze fell on the steps near the edge of the garden.

There, a frail dandelion stood. It had sprouted from a crack in the concrete, its leaves yellowed and brittle. Yet its slender stalk remained upright, bearing two or three small but resolute flowers. One had already transformed into fluffy white seeds, whispering softly in the faint breeze.

"Is that you, Dandelion?" I crouched down, my voice tinged with hesitant familiarity.

The dandelion swayed gently, as if nodding in reply.

"It's me, my friend," it rasped, its voice dry yet joyful. "You've come."

I looked down at it and softly asked, "How have you been? Are you doing well?"

"Not bad," the dandelion replied with a light chuckle, its flowers trembling in the wind. "Though the soil here is scarce, I've carved out my own little patch. Look, I'm still blooming, and my children are nearly ready to take flight. Soon, like me, they'll drift away with the wind to find new horizons."

"Have you found the star you were searching for?" I asked.

The dandelion paused, lifting its gaze toward the neon glow of the city. Its voice turned pensive. "When I first arrived here, I thought these lights were stars—my long-cherished dream. But I soon realized this place wasn't what I had imagined."

"Why not?" I pressed gently.

"The hardness of the concrete, the barrenness of the soil—it made me doubt if I could even survive. Sunlight only filters through the shadows of towering buildings, and the dust-laden wind makes it hard to breathe. In my early days here, I often questioned myself, sometimes even wept. I tried so hard to root myself, but everything seemed to reject me, mocking me as if I'd never bloom again."

I reached out to touch its leaves, hoping to offer comfort.

The dandelion swayed lightly, shaking its head as it continued, "In those dark moments, I thought about giving up.

Drifting endlessly, I felt lost, unsure of what to do next. Even staying alive seemed difficult. But as I anchored myself in the soil, drawing every drop of water I could find, savoring the rare rays of sunshine, I told myself, 'Just a little more. Try a little longer. As long as I'm alive, I'll keep growing.'

"Over time, I realized that chasing stars isn't about the perfect ending. It's about living in the moment, striving with all my heart. It's the act of dreaming and yearning, of pressing forward with hope, that makes life so precious."

I looked at it, my emotions swirling. "But didn't you lose the sunlight, the rain, and all the friends in the forest by chasing these stars? Do you regret it?"

The dandelion gazed at me, its petals faintly glowing under the neon lights.

"Perhaps," it said softly, its voice filled with gentle resolve. "In the forest, there was sunlight, rain, and soft earth. But look—" its flower swayed slightly, "this vibrant life is my star. Every choice comes with gain and loss. Comparing some-one else's gain to your own loss only brings pain. The journey of chasing my dreams has given me purpose and mean-ing."

Its words left me in quiet contempla-tion. I stared at its upright stalk, my eyes following the seeds as they floated away, like tiny travelers carrying hope into the unknown.

The dandelion swayed gently, whisper-ing to me, "Go now, star-chasing traveler. Set forth."

I took a deep breath, slowly stood, and began walking toward the edge of the city.

The sun dipped below the horizon, casting long streaks of twilight across the sky. I turned back for one last glance. There it stood, steadfast in its crack in the concrete, its flowers blooming against the odds.

"Farewell, Dandelion," I whispered, lift-ing my hand in a gentle wave.

A lone fluffy seed drifted down from its flower, following me as if to accompany me on my journey—brave and resolute, just like the dandelion itself once was.

I stepped into the darkness of the city.

The road ahead remained uncertain, but within my heart, a quiet strength had begun to grow.

SIX

THE MONSTER

Night descended, carrying a touch of chill in the air.

I curled up inside the hollow of an ancient tree, the fallen leaves beneath me soft and comforting. Shadows from the tree branches danced across the moonlit ground, and the moonlight itself streamed through the crevices of the hollow, caressing my face like a gentle veil.

Suddenly, I noticed two bluish-purple points of light flickering at the top of the hollow, reminiscent of playful stars in the night sky. Curious, I sat up and looked around.

A mischievous voice called out from above, "Are you here to catch me, hunter?"

Startled, I instinctively leaned back. "Hunter? What's a hunter? I used to be someone trapped in a box, and now, I'm a seeker of stars."

"Whoosh—"

A shadow darted down from the top of the hollow, circling around me several times before landing lightly in front of me.

I could finally make out its figure: a small black, curly-furred monster, its body soft and endearing like a fluffy kitten. Its large eyes sparkled, as if containing an entire galaxy of blue and purple. Perched atop its head were two crimson horns, and a pair of semi-transparent black wings lightly fluttered on its back, ethereal yet powerful.

I slowly sat down to meet its gaze. In a soft voice, I asked, "Who are you?"

It narrowed its gleaming eyes, lifting its chin proudly. "I am Kongjing, a little monster from the Abyss. I have the power to reflect people's hearts. Many hunters desire to capture me—they want to cut off my wings to make a potion, grind my red horns into powder for their spells, and chain me with bells to turn me into a pitiful house cat."

I furrowed my brow and murmured, "That's horrible... I've seen a world bound by chains. Those people view freedom as dangerous and chains as safe. They're even obsessed with imposing chains on those who are free."

The little monster's eyes lit up, and it smiled. "You're an interesting person! I like what you said. I, too, detest those who try to tame me. I am a child of the Abyss, a beast born to fly free."

Its wings fluttered lightly, and its voice carried a trace of pride. "Those so-called 'hunters'—they can make me suffer, they can even bring me death, but they can never take away my freedom. Death is merely the beginning of rebirth, and I've been reborn countless times in the Abyss."

I hesitated for a moment and then asked gently, "Would you tell me your stories about the hunters?"

The little monster stared at me and sniffed lightly. "Your scent is strange. You carry strong desires, yet you're surprisingly clean... Never mind. Stories of hunters are too murky for a pure-hearted child like you."

It folded its wings and gave a soft smile. "Close your eyes. Tonight, I'll visit your dreams and tell you a gentle tale."

Finding a comfortable position, I closed my eyes.

The little monster's voice echoed in my ears:

"I'm already in your dream. Don't be afraid; listen as I tell you my story."

The dream world unfolded, and I found myself in the Abyss.

Its depths shifted and morphed, never remaining in one place. Sometimes it nestled deep in a forest, sometimes on a cold and jagged mountaintop, or under the dazzling neon lights of a city, in a shadowy alleyway, within someone's obsessive mind, or at the bottom of a lonely and mad heart.

In those moments, I would traverse the Abyss, peeking into people's desires, reflecting their unattainable dreams with my empty mirror. Their desires and dreams were often bitter and hard to digest. Consuming them was always a painful ordeal.

But one day, the Abyss paused in a vast grassland. This was rare, as grasslands were sparsely populated, making food scarce. As I wandered through the night, all I saw was a flock of sheep and a shepherd sleeping alone under the stars.

Its voice softened, as though recounting a distant memory:

"That night, I crept closer to the shepherd's wooden cabin, ready to peek into his dreams. But just as I approached, he woke up and grabbed my foot."

"We stared at each other in the darkness, neither of us speaking.

Finally, I broke the silence with a soft 'Hey.'

He replied, equally softly, 'Hey.'

'Who are you?'

'I am the shepherd here.'

'A shepherd?'

'Yes. As a shepherd, I am the king of this grassy kingdom. My subjects are the sheep, obedient and docile, always following my command.'

'That sounds impressive, but managing so many sheep seems like a heavy burden.'

'Of course. A king has responsibilities and duties. But I am content and happy. Perhaps someday, I'll find a clever sheepdog from a neighboring kingdom to help me manage the flock. And you? Where are you from, and where are you going?'

'I am Kongjing, a little monster from the Abyss, here to harvest your desires and dreams. Aren't you afraid of me?'

The shepherd chuckled, his laughter shaking his body. 'Ah, yes, so terrifying! Absolutely terrifying!'

And so, the shepherd and I laughed together, and our story began."

By day, he herded his sheep across the plains. By night, he sat quietly in his wooden cabin, waiting for my arrival. I told him stories of the Abyss, fragments of dreams, and clouds of desires floating above the city's skyline. He told me about the grasslands, herding sheep, taming horses, and his visions of the future.

His desires were simple and pure, unable to satiate my hunger but unlike anything I had ever tasted before—sweet, light, and warm.

I found joy in them, and every night, I returned.

I watched him grow from a boy to a man, saw him grow strong and resolute, saw him conscripted into the king's army and march off to a holy war.

I located the Abyss' nodes, occasionally peeking out to check if he had returned. His sheep were scattered, and wild grass grew wildly. His small wooden house fell into disrepair, the wind carrying an air of desolation. His face grew blurred in my memory, his figure faint, yet my longing for him persisted—a tiny, unbreakable red thread connecting me to him.

One day, he returned at last, clad in battered armor and bearing scars that told stories of pain. His face was weathered, his gaze colder.

He removed his armor and donned the soft garments of a shepherd, rebuilding his tiny, dilapidated cabin. But each night, nightmares woke him, his hand trembling as it traced the scars left on his body.

I appeared silently before him, looking into his eyes—eyes that shifted from fear and wariness to a gentle warmth.

Yet, he no longer spoke as he once did. His gaze carried pain and struggles I couldn't comprehend.

And so, our tale continued: I shared stories of the outside world, strange and ancient tales, while he sat silently, lost in thought."

The little monster smiled at me, its voice gentle and mysterious:

"Traveler, day has broken. Wake up."

I opened my eyes, sunlight streaming through the tree hollow, warming my face.

"You must set out again."

And so, I began walking again, the road ahead illuminated by the faint glow of stars.

SEVEN

THE CHAMELEON

The morning breeze, carrying the crispness of the sunlight, gently caressed my face.

I slowly opened my eyes, rubbing the sleep from them. Weak sunlight filtered through the entrance of the hollow, and I saw a figure sitting on a rock at the opening, their legs swinging lazily as they faced away from me.

I called out, "Kongjing? Why have you taken on the appearance of a human?"

The person turned their head. Their yellow eyes widened slightly, and their small body, wrapped in a dull gray linen outfit, seemed to mirror my own. Their round face, tinged with a hint of confusion, puffed slightly, and their short black hair clung to their forehead. They looked just like me.

"Who are you? Why do you look just like me?" I rubbed my eyes quickly, staring hard. I realized that they were no longer "me" but instead a chameleon, their body covered in textured, scale-like patterns.

"You're not human. You're a chameleon. I've read about your features and descriptions before."

The creature laughed, a hint of surprise in its voice. "You can see through my disguise? Not many can do that. Most people assume they've met another version of themselves."

It extended a clawed hand, pointing to its scales. "Yes, I am a chameleon who disguises myself as a human to protect myself."

"Why did you choose to look like me?" I frowned, my small brows furrowing in confusion.

"Because humans are always partial to things that resemble themselves," the chameleon said, its eyes growing deep and thoughtful. "By mimicking you, I ensure my safety. When I meet an angel, I become an angel; when I meet a demon, I become a demon; when I meet a philosopher, I become a philosopher; and when I meet a beggar, I become a beggar. Humans are selfish—they love and protect what reflects 'themselves' the most."

"That's an incredible transformation. I don't have such magic," I said earnestly. "I'm just a lonely seeker of stars."

The chameleon fixed me with a faint smile, its expression unreadable. "But as a philosopher-chameleon, I must ask you: Are you truly seeking the stars, or are you seeking yourself? Who are the stars? Are they you? And who are you?"

"You're speaking in riddles! I don't understand at all," I said, scratching my head in confusion. "But you're so clever and magical—you must be amazing!"

The chameleon burst into laughter, its tail lightly slapping the rock. "Of course, unless I meet someone who wishes to harm themselves."

"How could anyone want to harm themselves?" I asked, my voice sincere. "I worked so hard to leave the box I lived in, to step out into this world. I've felt the wind's touch, seen vivid flowers, and embarked on a mysterious road toward the stars. It's lonely sometimes, but it's a journey full of hope."

The chameleon regarded me silently before smiling softly. It reached into its pocket and produced two small, crimson berries, handing one to me. "Here, take this—it's the 'Berry of Clarity.' Ahead of you are two paths: one filled with mud and thorns, and the other lined with blooming flowers, though the latter conceals dangerous man-eating plants. If you eat this berry, you won't be deceived by the man-eating flowers or harmed by the thorns."

I accepted the berry, turning it over in my hands with curiosity. "Did you come from the thorny path?"

The chameleon shook its head, a trace of pride in its expression. "No, chameleons can change endlessly. When I can't decide, I split into two selves, sending each down a different path. As long as one of 'me' survives, I continue living."

"Did both of you make it out alive?" I asked, clutching the berry tightly.

The chameleon licked its lips, a glint of fear passing through its eyes. "I barely survived the man-eating flowers. You must know, they're incredibly beautiful—born deceivers and masters of disguise. They take the form of what you desire most, drawing you in until you can't escape. Then, they open their jaws and swallow you whole."

The chameleon smiled faintly, its pride returning. "But I'm no ordinary creature. I might be the first to escape the clutches of the man-eating flowers. The 'me' who ventured into their field returned with these berries. The 'me' who braved the thorns was scratched and torn but also survived. Together, we rejoined and became whole again."

I widened my eyes in awe. "What do the man-eating flowers look like? Why are they so dangerous?"

The chameleon's expression turned solemn, and it spoke in a low voice. "The man-eating flowers are beautiful, romantic, and enchanting. Like me, they're born deceivers.

"Sometimes, they masquerade as wandering poets, singing irresistible songs to lure their prey, only to reveal their toothy maws.

"Sometimes, they appear as injured birds, transforming into grotesque demons the moment you approach.

"And sometimes, they become what you most desire—redemption, hope, kindness, love, even your true self. But at their core, they are fear, lies, emptiness, arrogance, and self-doubt. Only by consuming their victims can they briefly feel fulfilled, blooming in their most dazzling form."

The chameleon sighed, continuing, "Why did I approach them, you ask? Because I had never truly seen myself. When I saw a flower, I became a flower; when I saw a lake, I became a lake; when I saw a bird, I became a bird. Even when I looked in a mirror, I became the mirror itself. And mirrors reflecting mirrors yield only emptiness."

"But in the illusions of the man-eating flowers, I saw myself. I saw my forked tongue, my coarse scales, and my awkward legs. It was overwhelming—half of me wanted to look away from my ugliness, while the other half longed to see myself fully, to affirm my existence. But as I leaned closer, I nearly lost my life."

"In the final moment, I woke up. Why did I need such clarity? Overly sharp self-awareness only brings unbearable pain. All I needed was to accept that I am an imperfect chameleon—and that brought me more peace than I'd ever known."

"And so, I transformed into a man-eating flower. While it raged in its own illusions, I seized its berries and escaped."

Listening intently, I took a bite of the berry. Its juice ran down my chin, sweet yet tinged with bitterness. A surge of warmth coursed through my body, making me cough, but I managed to hold it in.

After a moment of reflection, I said, "You didn't want me to take that path because I have something I deeply want, right? A glowing star—a dream. And because of that, I'm susceptible to the kind of illusion where it seems I can achieve it instantly."

"Thank you for the berry, Chameleon," I continued earnestly. "And thank you for teaching me. Please believe me—you are worthy of your own love. You are not a flower, not a bird, not a lake, and not a mirror. You are simply yourself. I can see your scales and forked tongue clearly, and I also see the shimmering blue and green on your scales. They aren't ugly—they're beautiful."

The chameleon froze momentarily, a softness flickering in its eyes. Slowly, it transformed back into its true form: rough scales, a forked tongue, and four solid, unwavering legs.

It glanced at itself, then back at me, offering a gentle smile before turning to leave.

I watched its retreating figure until it vanished, perhaps becoming a plant or an animal once more.

Standing up, I moved toward the fork in the road, catching a glimpse of the golden glow of the man-eating flower field in the distance—a light eerily reminiscent of stars. But I was not swayed and resolutely chose the thorny path.

Curiously, the thorns did not pierce my feet.

I thought to myself, though my journey is fraught with danger, it is also filled with beauty and complexity. Like the red berry the chameleon gave me, sweet yet bitter, resting warmly in my stomach.

EIGHT

THE WEAVER

I continued along the road ahead when I saw a figure moving toward me, pausing and bending down occasionally. As I got closer, I realized it was a girl made of earth.

She looked to be around seven or eight years old. Her body, formed from soil, was covered with dry cracks. Embedded in her surface were stones of various colors, along with branches and leaves. She moved slowly, her head perpetually bowed, her back slightly hunched, like an old woman, inching forward in silence. Every few steps, she bent down to pick up a red stone, pulled out a small water bottle from her bag, and poured a little water into the cracks near her heart. Then, with a furrowed brow, she pressed the stone firmly into place.

I watched her as she finished, seemingly exhausting all her strength, before sitting quietly by the roadside. I approached and sat across from her on the opposite side of the road, observing her in silence.

For a long time, she seemed oblivious to my presence, her empty gaze fixed on the ground.

Unable to contain myself, I softly said, "Hi, hello."

Startled, she looked up, and small red stones appeared on her face, as if forming a blush. In a quiet, hesitant voice, she said, "I'm fine—no, hello. Who are you? When did you sit here?"

"Sorry for scaring you," I said gently. "I used to live in a box, but now I'm a seeker of stars. I've been sitting here for about fifteen minutes."

"It's okay. My soul is incomplete, so if I don't focus hard enough, I can't see other people. I don't even know who I am. All I know is that I'm piecing together my soul."

"Piecing together your soul? Why do you need to piece it together?" I asked, puzzled.

"My body is my soul, and my soul is my body," she replied. "When I can't adapt to the sun's passion, I crack all over. When I can't handle the wind's pursuit, it blows away my hair and nose. When I can't bear the rain's fury, I shrink and feel small and unworthy."

I asked, "So how can you heal both your body and your soul?"

She shook her head. "I don't know. But as I walk, I find different stones that feel like pieces of my soul. I pick them up, clean them, and place them into my body."

"How many pieces of your soul have you pieced together? You seem like a complete earthen figure to me, just with a few cracks."

She thought for a moment and then said, "There's still a part of my soul that's lost, scattered, and anxious. It's this unease and blur that keeps me breaking apart and mending myself again and again. I've even thought about using human glue from the towns to stick myself together, but I worry that I'll end up smelling like glue—a stinky, sticky person."

I asked, "What are you uneasy about?"

She replied, "I've been to many places and met many people. In some places, people think I'm a monster. They use cruel words to attack me and try all sorts of ways to drive me away. It makes me feel small and afraid. In other places, people think I'm a deity. They want to imprison me and worship me. That makes me arrogant but also afraid. These extreme reactions have torn me apart. I don't know what I truly am."

I looked at her, and she looked back at me. I saw her eyes fill with tears, and in their glistening surface, I saw my own reflection. Somehow, my eyes also welled up with tears.

Softly, I said, "In your eyes, I see my reflection. In my eyes, you'll find yours. Through me, you can see who you are.

Just as I see in your eyes a weary traveler, a curious and pure-hearted child, dandelions and fireflies, cats and bushes, and a sky full of stars. What do you see in mine?"

She stood up and walked closer to me. Sitting across from me, she leaned in, gazing intently into my eyes. In a gentle voice, she said, "I see the earth that carries all things, the colorful stones, the rivers and the passage of history, life dying and reviving, birds' old nests, leaves falling in autumn, snow in winter, and seeds silently taking root in the cracks."

She clapped her hands and laughed, her face lighting up. "So this is who I am."

Tears rolled down my cheeks.

Her eyes sparkled with life, and she said happily, "Yes, this is who I am—not beautiful or ugly, not a monster or a deity. I don't need to feel small, nor do I need to feel superior. I'm just myself. Thank you for helping me see myself. Now I can finally become a complete soul!"

She opened her bag and poured all the water she had into her cracks. I watched as green grass began to grow rapidly, filling in the gaps. She started to dance, moving through the earth, diving in and out of the soil. Finally, she plucked a small flower and placed it gently in my hand.

Then she merged with the earth and disappeared.

I hugged myself and cried, though I wasn't sure why.

I thought, maybe she was the earth itself.

I thought, maybe she had seen herself.

I thought, maybe I had seen myself too.

NINE

THE TREE

The blazing sun beat down on me, leaving my throat parched and my body weary. Ahead of me lay a three-way intersection. I had come down one path, and now two roads branched off in opposite directions. At the center of the crossroads stood a massive tree. Its lush branches spread out like an open green umbrella, casting dappled patterns of light and shadow onto the ground. The sturdy trunk rose skyward as if trying to touch the heavens, while the wide canopy stretched outward, shading both paths in its embrace.

"Rustle, rustle... O weary traveler, come rest beneath my shade," the tree seemed to sing softly as its leaves swayed gently in the breeze. Startled, I walked toward the tree and sat on one of its gnarled, raised roots. Cool shadows enveloped me, and one by one, fruits dropped from the tree, landing neatly at my feet.

"Thank you, great tree, for your shade and your fruit," I said, looking up in gratitude.

"Thank you, traveler," the tree's voice resonated warmly from its leaves, deep and soothing. "It has been so very long since anyone paused here, willing to share a moment with me."

I blinked, surprised, and tilted my head toward the majestic tree. "So long? Have there been other travelers on this road?"

The tree swayed its branches lightly, its voice tinged with the softness of reminiscence. "Yes, many lonely travelers have passed by here, just like you. Long ago, I was but a small sapling, silently growing at this crossroads. My roots stretched deep into the soil, watching countless travelers pass. And then one day, she came."

"She?" I asked, intrigued.

"Yes, a girl who lingered at the crossroads, torn between paths. Her eyes held a mix of confusion and longing for the horizon. I was drawn to her—a feeling I could not put into words stirred within me, making me yearn to become something more. So, I hid my true form and transformed into a young boy. I approached her."

"Did she believe you?" I asked.

"She had no reason to doubt," the tree sighed wistfully. "I sat with her at the crossroads, and we talked of stars in the sky and stories of the earth. By twilight, she smiled and told me this was the most peaceful moment of her journey. She said perhaps we could walk the next part of the road together. In that instant, I thought I had found happiness."

The tree's voice grew quieter. "But then night fell, and a sudden storm broke. Rain soaked her hair, and she frowned in her sleep. At that moment, a powerful impulse surged within me—I wanted to shield her from the storm, to keep her by my side forever."

"And then?" I urged softly.

"My hands became branches, my feet turned into roots, and my body transformed into a massive trunk, digging deep into the earth. I poured all my strength into becoming a great tree, stretching my branches wide to shield her from the rain."

"When morning came, she woke and searched for me, calling my name with a voice full of worry and loss. I wanted to tell her I was right there, but I could no longer speak. All I could do was watch as she lingered beneath my shade before eventually shouldering her pack and continuing her journey."

"She didn't know you had become this tree?"

The tree was silent for a moment before speaking again, its voice heavy with reflection. "She thought we were fellow travelers on the same path. Even though I disguised myself as a traveler, I was always just a tree. I was destined to grow upward, while she was destined to move forward."

"Perhaps, to her, my sudden disappearance felt like rejection or abandonment. At the time, I believed her departure meant she lacked devotion to me. But now I understand—trying to control or interfere with someone else's journey stems from selfish desire, not love."

The tree's leaves rustled softly, as if in self-mockery. "After she left, I grew as tall as I could, as strong as I could. I thought, if I became big enough, tall enough, then maybe one day, as she walked her path and looked up, she'd see me. She'd remember that at this crossroads, there was once a tree that stood silently, always watching over her."

"And," the tree added, its voice tender, "I hoped to grow tall enough to see farther—to catch glimpses of her, even as her figure faded into the distance. To keep watch over her, even if all I could see was a tiny shadow."

I lifted my gaze to the towering crown of the tree. The sunlight filtering through its leaves painted a delicate patchwork of light and shadow, like the tree's gentle eyes.

"Great tree, your strength isn't just for her—it's also for yourself. You've protected her, and you've sheltered other travelers too. Love isn't about possession; it's about allowing others the freedom to become themselves."

The tree's leaves rustled, a sound like an affirming sigh, or perhaps a soft, grateful song.

"Thank you, traveler," the tree murmured. "You are the first to sit and listen to my story."

I smiled and replied, "You're welcome. And thank you."

I sat on the tree's roots, finding a moment of peace under its protective canopy. As twilight deepened and darkness crept over the land, I looked up at the sky, now adorned with the faint glow of stars. I knew my journey was far from over.

"Thank you, great tree. I must go now," I said softly, rising to my feet and walking toward the distant starlight.

The tree's leaves swayed gently in the breeze, as if bidding me farewell or continuing its silent vigil.

TEN

THE DEITY

Night fell completely, and before me stretched a vast wasteland. The eerie silence was almost oppressive. Dead trees, like twisted arms, reached toward the blackened sky. Flocks of black crows perched on the branches, occasionally letting out hoarse cries, adding to the desolation and loneliness.

As I walked through this barren expanse, the wind carried grains of sand that lashed against my face. I felt both chilled and alone.

Suddenly, a faint tremor rippled through the wasteland.

The goddess said, "I shall appear."

And so, she did.

I stopped in my tracks and saw her leaning casually against a withered tree. She stood barefoot, her soles covered in soil and healed scars. The wind and sand flowed between us, whispering mournfully. I approached her and sat quietly beside her on the tree's gnarled roots. As we both looked downward, the ground beneath us began to shimmer, forming a small pool of water. Within it, like a carousel, countless images of human lives played out: I saw lonely travelers walking their own paths, meeting people and events, weaving stories as they journeyed.

I turned to her and asked softly, "Goddess, as you lower your eyes to observe human suffering, is it indifference or compassion that you feel?"

She smiled faintly and brushed her hand through my hair. Her touch was gentle yet carried a timeless weight. In her smile, I glimpsed exhaustion and mercy, like a traveler burdened by countless ages and sorrows.

"The goddess, too, did not understand the stories of the mortal world at first," she said with a sigh, her gaze drifting toward the farthest reaches of the wasteland.

After speaking, she rose slowly. Her cool fingertips lightly touched my brow.

In an instant, my vision blurred, and the world began to twist and shift. It felt as though some unseen force was pulling me into another realm. Just before my sight vanished completely, I caught a glimpse of her figure dissolving into a wisp of smoke and light, silently vanishing into the darkness.

"Seeker of the stars, if you wish to understand, then witness it yourself."

When I opened my eyes again, the world around me was utterly transformed.

The sky was a dim, somber gray. The ground beneath my feet was soft and damp, as if I were walking through a dream shrouded in mist. In the distance, a colossal stone castle loomed in the barren wasteland. It stood solitary and solemn, as though time itself had frozen around it. Cracks ran along its walls, where dried vines clung stubbornly, exuding an ancient, lonely aura.

As I stepped through the castle gates, a warm light replaced the cold desolation outside. Gentle sunlight streamed through the tall windows, dust motes drifting lazily in the beams like golden threads in a slowly flowing tapestry. In the courtyard, green grass grew silently. Shy mimosa plants trembled in the breeze, their buds softly opening and closing as though breathing.

I looked up and saw her lying quietly on a chaise longue in the courtyard. She no longer bore the weary appearance of the wasteland but seemed instead like a sleeping maiden. The sunlight traced her soft features, her lips curled in a serene smile. Her expression was tranquil and peaceful.

At that moment, I transformed into a black cat, leaping lightly onto the chaise. I curled up beside her and closed my eyes languidly. I could hear the steady rhythm of her breathing and feel the faint warmth radiating from her body. The scene seemed frozen in time, as if the flow of years had paused entirely.

But suddenly, a strange wind swept through, carrying a low, mournful sound. The air outside the courtyard grew heavy, and a song echoed from afar—a song both desolate and eternal, as though it carried the weight of infinite solitude.

The goddess opened her eyes slowly, her gaze tinged with both confusion and tenderness. She rose, her skirt brushing the courtyard grass, and walked barefoot toward the glowing threshold.

I followed her footsteps, watching as the world beyond the castle began to change. The woods turned black and barren, their branches resembling countless skeletal hands clawing at the darkness.

She stepped into the shadows, her figure flickering within the haunting melody. I saw her bare feet cut by sharp stones, crimson droplets falling to the ground, blooming into dark red flowers. Yet she did not falter, her eyes unwavering, as though pursuing an unreachable truth.

"That is the solitude of the goddess," her voice drifted back through the wind. "When I first walked among mortals, I too felt lost, tormented, and conflicted. I wanted to save everything, to bring warmth to every living being. But I learned that even a goddess is but a traveler, walking through life with her own scars."

She stopped at the edge of a dense fog, turning slightly to look at me. Her eyes held boundless gentleness. "Seeker of the stars, solitude is not to be feared. It is through this solitude that we find light in the darkness and growth in the midst of pain."

The goddess spoke, "**All has ended, and all has yet to begin.**"

She transformed into a beam of light, piercing through the fog and vanishing into the distance.

When I returned to myself, I was once again standing in the wasteland.

I had returned to my journey, seeking the stars.

A cold wind swept past, and the crows took flight in unison, their harsh cries carrying away the last traces of silence. Yet my heart felt calm, as though a pair of warm hands had smoothed its edges.

I raised my eyes to the horizon, where the stars still shimmered faintly, like countless tiny flames guiding me through the darkness.

For some reason, I no longer felt like a solitary traveler.

Stars, I have come for you.

And one day, others will journey toward me.

AFTERWORD

This book began in 2022 and took two years to complete, written in fragments of reflection and emotion. Each word felt like a conversation with my soul, touching on love, growth, freedom, and direction—the eternal pursuits of life.

We are all on the journey of chasing stars. Perhaps someone may falter along the way, even fall, but there will always be others who rise and continue the path toward the stars. The characters in this book are those I've met, reflections of myself, and echoes of every soul striving to chase their dreams.

As I finished writing this book, I realized it's not just the end of a story but the culmination of a journey within. To you, the reader, I hope these words resonate with your heart and remind you of your own star—waiting for you to rise and reach it.

A solitary path, the stars far away,
Through biting winds and shadows gray.
A glimmer above, faint and bright,
A spark in the void, a guiding light.
At journey's end, the stars still call,
Feet weary and sore, but I'll never fall.
Some will falter, and some will rise,
Each light reflecting human ties.
As I gaze upon the eternal sky,
The stars respond with a gentle reply.
"Stars, I have come," I whisper to the night,
Knowing one day, others will follow my light.